Get Off Your Phone

The No Phone Zone

Written by
Natalie Kristen F. Carricarte

Story Creator:
Aimee Sheeber Knight

Archway Publishing books may be ordered through booksellers or by contacting:

Archway Publishing
1663 Liberty Drive
Bloomington, IN 47403
www.archwaypublishing.com
1 (888) 242-5904

ISBN: 978-1-4808-7249-3 (sc)
ISBN: 978-1-4808-7247-9 (hc)
ISBN: 978-1-4808-7248-6 (e)

Print information available on the last page.

Archway Publishing rev. date: 01/22/2020

Natalie Kristen F. Carricarte's Dedication

To my Beautiful kids, Nathaniel and
Savannah (Giddy) Carricarte.
You challenge me in awesome ways and I thank you
for helping me realize my dreams. I love you both for
your individuality and by Amazing me every day.
I also love my "other kids". You all know who you are!!!
Thank you to Kristin Carlson for
helping with creative edits.

Aimee Sheeber Knight's Dedication

I'd like to dedicate this book to my two children
Gia and Elijah and my husband Eric Knight. I wish
for them the simplicity and reward of really
seeing people and new horizons first hand.

This is a story of

how great life can be
when we spend
less time on cell phones
or watching TV.
Chatting at dinner
is something that was.
Now we type and we text,
and our cell phones go buzz.

Technology has changed us.
My dear, it's severe.
Devices are consuming
our entire atmosphere.

Phones ring-a-ding
every second of the hour.
Please tell me something, children—
who's giving them their power?

There's beauty in our differences,
like diamonds and white pearls.
Please allow me to introduce
two extremely different girls.

Meet techie Haddy Paddy
and outdoorsy Olive Green.
They're upside down
and right side up;
I'll show you what I mean.

Olive's family lives
just a minute up the road.
They don't mind squirmy worms
or gooey, warty toads.

A simpler life fulfills the Greens.
They farm sweet corn and lima beans.

The Greens' kids love to hang outside,
to fish and swim and surf the tide.
When grown-up neighbors stop to chat,
they know their names; wow, how 'bout that?

Do the Greens have cell phones?
Yes, of course they do.
They're just not super stuck to them,
like tubes of sticky glue.

The Greens would rather study stars
and name the constellations.
They seek deep friendships and not the web
for social validation.

Most nights you'll find the Paddys,
a very techie group,
separated on computers,
not together eating soup.

Mrs. Paddy reads online,
turning pages with a tap.
Mrs. Green reads aloud
with kiddos on her lap.

The husbands too, or so it seems,
are cut from different cloth.
Mr. Paddy tries new fads,
while Mr. Green likes classic plaid—
and coffee without froth.

If Haddy loses Internet,
she's quickly bored to tears.
She squirms and frets and starts to stress,
when facing real-life peers.

Mrs. Sunny smiles and says,
"Kids, no social noise.
Play outside this winter break.
Have fun now, girls and boys."
Haddy pleads, "This isn't fair.
I cannot bear. I'll lose my hair!"

"Haddy Paddy, you must not fret.
There's more to life than the Internet.
You will not lose your gorgeous hair."
Olive groaned in crazed despair.

"Olive Green, what do you know?
You play outside in frozen snow."
Haddy growled, her arms crossed tight.
"Perhaps you'll cook some corn tonight!"

These two girls differ. Do you see?
Haddy's techie as can be,
but Olive dreams of sled and skis.

Olive's hair is pulled up tight.
Haddy wears hers down.
It doesn't mean they're wrong or right;
they just need common ground.

What will happen? Do you know?
Will Olive play out in the snow?
Will Haddy text all winter break?
Please read on, for goodness' sake.

The first day of the break, Haddy broke Mrs. Sunny's rule.

She didn't even think about the silly rule from school.
Haddy started texting while eating chocolate cake.
The Wi-Fi petered out, so she raced to fix the break.
But in her frantic, harried haste, she made a rather huge mistake.

Her brother Sam, who saw the mess, said, "The milk is everywhere!"
He noticed that poor Chubbs the cat had icing in his hair.

"Uh-oh, Haddy, here comes Daddy.
You're in trouble now.
Mommy's desk is white with milk.
Did you spill a whole-stein cow?"

(Do you know what a whole-stein—
or Holstein—cow is?)

But Haddy begged him, "Please don't rat;
just play outside with Chubbs the cat."

"Dad will see it wasn't me;
My phone made the mistake.
It's hard to text with just one hand.
Come on … give me a break!

"Besides, I'm sure I've made Mom proud.
I sent our selfies to the cloud.
I'll hashtag this and hashtag that,
unlike the Greens' outdoorsy brat!"

A glitchy email came Dad's way.
Super loud they heard him say,
"My computer's acting really strange.
What happened to our Wi-Fi range?
Haddy Paddy, you've done it now!
You've fried our circuits. Tell me how!
It'll take forever to get this fixed.
The cloud can't hold that many pics."

With no Internet service for the night,
the Paddys couldn't function.
So they caught an airline flight
and headed to Grand Junction.

On bumpy roads the Paddys trekked.
But Daddy's texting caused a wreck.
They took the car in for repair,
hailed a cab, then paid the fare.

They got to the airport late that night.
"Where is Sam?" Mom shook with fright.

"I see Sam." Haddy pointed.
"He's at the charging station."
His eyes were locked upon his screen
in awestruck concentration.
His headphones sat upon his head
He leaned against the wall.
With so many darn distractions,
he'd missed their flight's last call.

Haddy yelled, "Run, Sammy, run!
They're closing up our gate.
The plane doesn't care; the plane won't wait.
Sam, if you don't hurry,
we'll never leave this state!"

The airline attendant,
a serious lady named Fern,
flashed a very angry look
and then seemed very stern.

"What were you doing?
What made you delay?"
Sam stared at his tablet
and then looked away.

"I was playing video games—
you know, looking down."
"Oh, what a shame," she said,
pretending with a frown.
"You'll have plenty of time to play games.
You're stuck here on the ground."

"But it's winter break," Haddy cried
and lifted her arched brow,
"Our plane's left town.
What the heck do we do now?

"A week, they said, for Wi-Fi.
Don't you even care?
We have to find a place to stay,"
she said and grabbed Sam's hair.

With their plans up in the air,
even Mom looked quite a mess.
Her eyes were disappointed,
and her face was red from stress.

Just when the Paddys thought
things could not get worse,
Haddy's mom pretended
to fumble through her purse.
"Don't look now," Mom whispered.
"OMG, we must be cursed."

Smiling, Mr. Green spoke up.
"Whoever could this be?"
A sarcastic Haddy mumbled,
"Oh noooo, it's Mr. Tree."

"Are you flying out tonight?"
asked Mr. Paddy kindly.
"Nope, just picking up our nana
from her home in Cincinnati."

But his daughter, Olive Green,
didn't stop for idle chatter.
She could see her neighbors' faces.
Something clearly was the matter.

To Haddy's amazed surprise,
Mr. Green was very wise.

"I saw you all so sad and blue.
But Olive knew what we should do.
We noticed you had missed your flight.
Come stay with us this blustery night."
"How 'bout it, Dad?" said little Sam.
"We'll eat pies and homemade jam."

Haddy spoke, pretending,
with crocodile tears.
"We haven't seen them for,
like, a hundred million years."
"It must be fate," Mr. Paddy said to his family.
"Thank you, dear Olive, for your hospitality."

At the house of Harold Green
were things that they had never seen—
a stereo on the mantelpiece and
fuzzy jackets lined with fleece.

But the next surprise—it made them shake
And fear they'd made a grave mistake.
Besides live plants—no way, no lie—
This house had life without Wi-Fi!

With all this downtime the Paddys had,
they found that offline wasn't bad.
In fact, an unplugged home could be
Super downright awesome.
They played ball with the dog
and watched their friendships blossom.

Instead of texting they talked out loud,
which made the Paddy parents proud.

And joy glowed in their high-tech hearts
to see kids laugh at low-tech farts!
Sam enjoyed this time inside;
he felt a sudden sense of pride.

"You know what, Haddy? This was fun,
Playing games and eating sticky buns.
"I think you're right," Haddy said.
"This was sweet.
"This power-down's been kind of neat."

Phones are great when we're apart.
But sharing our lives, heart to heart,
works better when we're face-to-face
and not zoned out in cyberspace.

Let's go for walks without our screens
and smell the crisp of evergreens.
We'll do more and try our best.
We'll just ignore our beeping texts.

We'll notice things like shooting stars
and no more texting in our cars.

Whether you're a Haddy Paddy
or an Olive Green,
make a garden filled with
love and lima beans.

Unplug your world.
You will not drown.
There's more to life
than looking down.
Play outside or read a book.
Choose a recipe to cook.

There's more to life
than pixelated screens.
Go outside;
Create new dreams.

Dear kiddos,
start by looking up.
Then talk to friends
and ask them, SUP?

The End

Dear friends,
It's so important to teach our children that cell phones are a privilege and a responsibility.

The Get Off Yer Phone series intends to open up children's minds and help them understand the important issues associated with social media.

We must equip our children with good, strong values and a better understanding of this technological world we live in today.
I give you the first book ...

GET OFF YOUR PHONE.

Printed in the United States
By Bookmasters